This book belongs to

_____

For Sam and Chloey
-J.F.

To Mom, Dad, Kayleigh,
Brooke, David, and Alaric
-K.A.

This is a book published by Puggers, LLC
Pug Story © 2012 by Jaclyn Fearheller
Designed and illustrated by Kyrstin Avello
Created and printed in the USA

First Edition, October 2012
ISBN 978-1-62407-214-7

Visit us on the web!
Pugstory.com

The sun's yellow glow was shining through the curtains. There was a bird chirping on the window sill. It was time for Chloey the Pug to wake up and start her day. She was living in a new house, in a new city, with a new park.

Chloey was four years old. The only home she had known was in San Francisco, where there were so many parks. And every walk meant going up and down at least three hills.

Chloey's recent move to Chicago raised so many questions: What will Chicago be like? Will the other dogs like me? Will I make new friends? Is there a park near my house?

Chloey climbed out of bed and stretched her legs. Her curly tail bounced back to its corkscrew-like shape. Her shiny tan coat did not have one hair out of place.

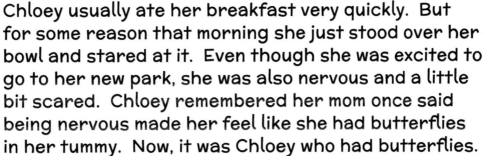

Chloey usually ate her breakfast very quickly. But for some reason that morning she just stood over her bowl and stared at it. Even though she was excited to go to her new park, she was also nervous and a little bit scared. Chloey remembered her mom once said being nervous made her feel like she had butterflies in her tummy. Now, it was Chloey who had butterflies.

Chloey decided not to let the fact that she was nervous and a little bit scared keep her from going out. So, she left on her adventure.

The rain had created HUGE puddles in the street but that didn't
seem to bother Chloey. Her nervous excitement showed.

She would run quickly and then stop.
Run quickly and then stop.

Chloey's velvety ears flopped wildly with each step.
Her pink tongue hung out because she was panting.

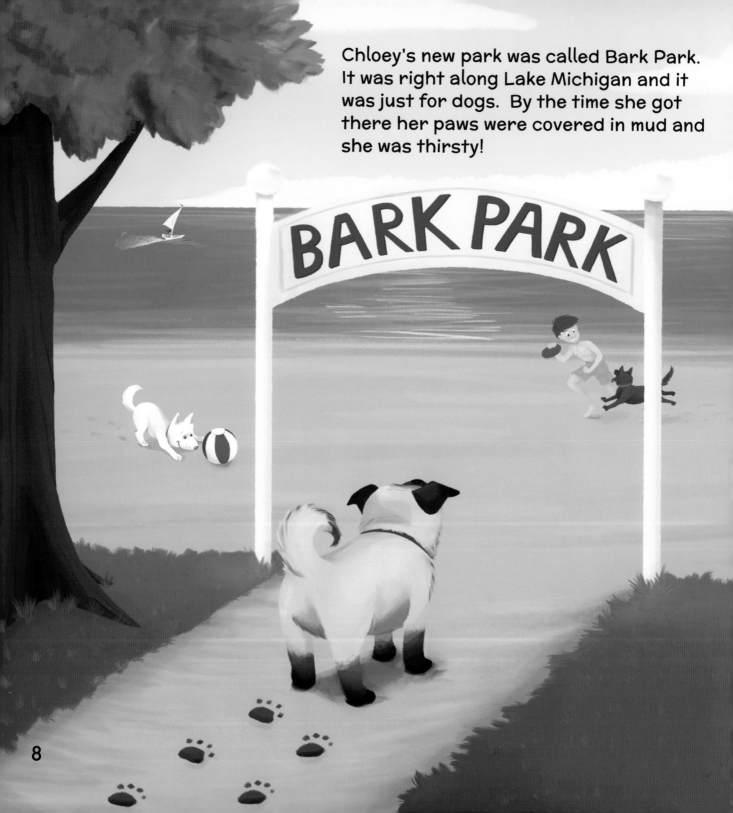

Chloey's new park was called Bark Park. It was right along Lake Michigan and it was just for dogs. By the time she got there her paws were covered in mud and she was thirsty!

8

Chloey looked around and found the water fountain. It was the coolest looking fountain for dogs Chloey had ever seen! She took a drink and then heard a gruff voice behind her say, "Hey, save some for the whales." It sounded like a GIANT talking.

"Huh?" she nervously replied.

"Lighten up kid, it's just an expression. There are no whales here. It means save some water for the rest of us. It's supposed to be funny."

"Oh," chuckled Chloey.

"That's better," said the Hound. "They call me Brutus. What's your name?"

"My name is Chloey. I'm new in town."

Just then a soccer ball came flying through the air and bonked Chloey right on the head. A very hyper Greyhound named Gracie ran over to get the ball and asked her if she was okay. Still seeing stars Chloey looked up and answered, "I'm ok."

Gracie looked relieved and ran back to the game with the ball.

"You gotta watch out for her," Brutus told Chloey. "It's like she has ants in her pants," he joked. "That girl never sits still."

Chloey watched the soccer game and wished she was playing. She loved soccer. It looked like the other dogs were having so much fun. Each dog was a different size, color, and breed.

All of a sudden a whistle blew and the game was over. The dogs started lining up to get picked for new teams. Chloey was scared that she might not get picked. What if they don't like me? she wondered. Determined to make new friends she walked over and got in line. She waited and hoped that she would get picked.

Chloey did not get picked. Maybe because she was new to the park or maybe it was because they already had enough players. The reason did not matter though. Her feelings were hurt. She felt like crying but held it back. Her curly tail straightened out as she left the park. Brutus saw what happened and shouted out to her.

On Chloey's way home she felt sad. She missed her old friends and wished she could play with them again. She pictured their familiar faces.

When Chloey got home her mom asked about her day.

"I've had better. I didn't get picked for soccer," Chloey told her.

"I'm so sorry. Did you meet any nice dogs?" her mom asked.

"I met a GIANT dog named Brutus."

"That's good honey," her mom said. Chloey didn't feel like talking or eating though. Her mom hugged her tightly and said, "Tomorrow is a new day."

As Chloey plopped into bed she felt as heavy as a raindrop hitting the pavement.

She was so tired and still felt sad. She laid in bed and thought about the last thing Brutus said to her.

Better luck next time, kid!

What did Brutus mean by that? she wondered.

All of a sudden it was like a light came on and Chloey understood what he meant. Even though she was disappointed about not getting picked for a team, she had to go back and try again.

Like her mom told her earlier that night, tomorrow is a new day.

There has to be a next time!

The next morning Chloey woke up and left the house earlier than
usual. As she walked back to Bark Park she still felt nervous like the
day before but she kept going.

After she walked into the park, she took a deep breath and looked around. There was a soccer game about to begin. Brutus saw her and yelled, "Hey kid, come get in line for the next game."

Powder, the Labrador, was counting everyone who wanted to play in the game. She was in charge. Powder was smart and counted very well. She finished counting an even number of dogs and announced, "EVERYONE PLAYS TODAY!"

Chloey was so excited!

1 2
3 4 5
6 7
8 9
10

The referee was an older dog named Dutchie. He was a Dachshund who took the game very seriously. Dutchie was a great referee because his legs were so short. He was the closest to the ground and could see everyone's paws very well. Dutchie was not afraid to call a time out or use his whistle. He blew it to start the game.

After Dutchie blew his whistle, the ball was kicked to Chloey. She trapped it with her paws and passed it to her teammate. The other dogs were surprised by how good she was.

23

The ball was passed back to Chloey. She used her back legs to kick the ball far and with great force. It was an amazing kick! It looked like a star shooting through the sky.

The ball went straight into the goal. Dutchie blew his whistle again and yelled, "GOAL!"

"HOORAY!" Chloey's teammates shouted.

Chloey was happy she scored a goal. She was even happier that she was making new friends. Going back to Bark Park was the right choice. Chloey did not feel nervous anymore and her butterflies were disappearing.

Chloey played a couple more games before it began to get dark. Time to head home for dinner, she thought. She said goodbye to her new friends and told them she would see them soon.

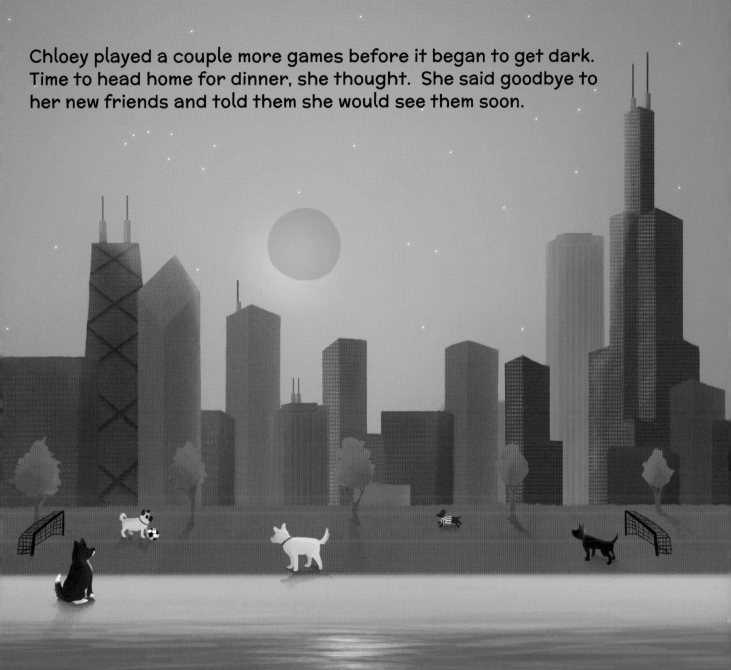

27

Chloey couldn't wait to tell her mom about her day!

"MOM, MOM!" she yelled as she ran in the door.

"Honey, what's going on?" her mom asked.

28

"I had the best day at Bark Park! I got picked for soccer and I made new friends. I got to know Brutus the Hound, Gracie the Greyhound, Powder the Labrador, and Dutchie the Dachshund. And, I scored a goal!"

"I am so proud of you, Chloey."

After dinner and story time, it was bedtime.

Chloey nestled into her soft bed and rolled onto her side. Her pink belly showed as she let out a sigh. What a day. Moving to Chicago was not that scary after all. My new home and friends are going to be great! she thought to herself. Chloey drifted off to sleep and dreamt about her new friends at Bark Park and all of their adventures to come.

THANK YOU!

Team Pug Story would like to pass along a heartfelt
thank you to our generous backers, loving families,
supportive friends, and of course, our readers.
It is because of people like you that
dreams come true!

CHLOeY'S Q & a

1. Did you like "Chloey's BIG Move"? ● Why or why not?

2. Have you ever moved to a new city? ● How did you feel?

3. What is the name of the city you live in now? ● What's your address?

4. Do you ever get "butterflies" in your tummy when you meet new people?

5. What is your favorite team activity to do with your friends?

6. Have you ever felt left out of a game before? ● How did you feel?

7. What are some things you can do to include new people in your activies?

8. What was it like when you started a new school? ● How did you feel?

9. Did Chloey make the right choice by going back to Bark Park? ● Why?

10. Are you excited for the next book to come out in the Pug Story series?

YOUR PAGE!

1. _____

2. _____

3. _____

4. _____

5. _____

6. _____

7. _____

8. _____

9. _____

10. _____

about us

Jaclyn Fearheller

Since moving back to Chicago from San Francisco 12 years ago with her Pugs, Jaclyn has been involved at the executive level for two companies that sell consumer products worldwide. A writer at heart, she has always wanted to create a book series that would help children and their parents tackle life's tough lessons. And now she has done it! Jaclyn resides in Chicago with her amazing husband and their beloved pets.

"In the last 15 years not a day has gone by where one of my Pugs or my niece and nephew has not made me smile simply by looking at them. I am finally able to combine my love of animals and passion for teaching children."

Kyrstin Avello

Kyrstin has earned a BFA in Media Arts and Animation, and currently works as a freelance artist. She has collaborated on a wide array of projects outside of Pug Story, including TV storyboards, character concepts, traditional paintings, and graphic design. A dog owner her entire life, Kyrstin resides in the Chicago suburbs, and is the happy owner of a Shiloh Shepherd named Blade.